INSEPARABLE

A Love That Never Ends

Sarita Walker

DEDICATION

To everyone who met their soul mate, only to lose them far too soon. The world is hard; the universe unending, and sometimes our lives don't come to the conclusion that we expected. But just as love is enduring, so too are we. With each step forward, it will be easier to make than the last.

Copyright Notice 2022 ©

All rights reserved. No part of this publication may be reproduced, distributed, or transmitted in any form or by any means, including photocopying, recording, or other electronic or mechanical methods without the prior written permission of the publisher, except in the case of brief quotations embodied in critical reviews and certain other non-commercial uses permitted by copyright law. Additionally, the publisher allows for non-profit fan fiction to be produced as long as the original text is clearly cited. 'Based on INSEPARABLE by Sarita Walker' will suffice. For permission requests, please contact the publisher.

ISBN (Paperback) 979-8-88895-590-1

Published by Sarita Walker

Copyright © 2022

For any request, please contact the publisher.

All rights reserved.

This is a work of fiction. Names, characters, businesses, places, events, locales, and incidents are either the products of the author's imagination or used in a fictitious manner. Any resemblance to actual persons, living or dead, or actual events is purely coincidental.

CHAPTER ONE

The Encounter
* *

It's supposed to be just any other day. I'm out here for work, making my way through the large, glass walled office building to handle some maintenance work. The idea is that I come in, I fix what needs to be fixed, and then I leave. It's an in and out job.
This is the kind of thing that I've done – well, only about a dozen times actually, considering that I haven't been working here for very long. Still, it's familiar.

But this time, something has caught my attention. There's a man on the inside of one of the offices that I need to get to. I'm checking out the monitor system that's hooked to the whole complex, and his room happens to have one.

I knock on the door, intruding myself as, "sent by maintenance."

The name tag that I'm wearing reads Jessica and the building security down on the first floor gave me a tag to wear that makes it obvious I'm supposed to be here. It also means that I don't have to try and introduce myself every five minutes, when someone new passes by. It's a Godsend at places like this, with half a dozen different offices shoved into the same building and several hundred people working in the place.

He looks over at me, all sharp blue eyes and strong jaw, his messy blonde hair pushed back out of his face. "Maintenance? Did the desk break without me knowing?"

"Not the desk." I gesture upwards, towards the alarm in the ceiling off to the corner of the room. "Just doing some basic checks, Mister."

I let the question hang, clearly fishing for a name. I'm half expecting him to reach forward and touch the golden placard on his desk like some of the other jerks that work in this place – as if no one ever sits at a coworkers desk to handle a problem, you know? I can read, I'm just making sure about who I'm talking to.

But instead, he just smiles and says, "David Holmes."

"Like the detective," I tease, with a little laugh. And then, waving a hand towards him, "Sorry, sorry, you probably get that one all the time."

"I get it often enough to not think it's a riot anymore," agrees David. "But coming from you, I don't mind it."

"Coming from me." I laugh and turn back to my work, setting the step ladder that I've brought in with me down on the ground and climbing up onto it; my feet thinking against the metal. I'm the kind of girl that wears tee shirts and jeans even when I'm not at work, so the tan khakis that I've got on fit me well. My hair is pulled back into a tight bun so it doesn't get in my face as I pull the tool kit from my belt and get to work, sliding it open and testing the features.

David does his own work as I go, his fingers tip tapping over the keyboard as he goes. It's not until I climb down from the step ladder that I realize the typing stopped a bit ago, and he's now staring at me.

"You just look so familiar," says David, in way of explanation.

I laugh and fold the step ladder back up, telling him, "I don't think that we've met. I never come out this way if it's not for a job – and honestly, I'm pretty new to the company. I've only been out this way a handful of times."

"Some other way, then," says David, with a hum. He continues to watch me as I put my gear back in order – and I'll be honest, I can't stop watching him, either. I know that there's something about him that's almost profound in nature. It's the sharpness in his eyes, the way it shudders down my spine when he tells me, "maybe we'll see each other again."

I can only hope so.

I don't stop thinking about David for the next two weeks, but it takes that long before I get a chance to actually see him again. The second time that we meet, it's not at his office building. He's putting in a system at his home, and I've been sent out to handle it.

It's a nice place on the good side of town, a lake front property that's totally fenced in, with a big white stone two floor building in the middle of it; a nice garden that lines the walkway. There's a screened in porch with white and blue wicker furniture on it, and when I knock on the door and David Holmes' opens it up, it feels like something slides into my throat and gets lodged there.

I've never been more caught off guard before in my entire life. I'm staring at him outside of his work clothes and it's like staring into the bright light. He's got on a white button up with the sleeves rolled up to the crooks of his elbows, and with no tie on, the top two buttons on the shirt are undone, showing off a peak of his chest.

It's electric.

It is not the norm when our eyes meet. The universe speaks in profound ways. Right now, it's speaking loudly, telling me that this is where we are supposed to be; that this is the perfect moment. There's a sharpness in his actions, the gestures of his hands, the way that he smiles when he invites me in.

David admits, "I asked for you specifically. I just really wanted to see you again. Is that weird?"

"It's a little weird," I tell him, but then I smile and finish, "but I'm glad that you did it anyway. I haven't been able to stop thinking about you."

He leads me through his house, showing me where he wants the alarms set. We chat the whole way and David explains to me that his father is a doctor – a famous neurosurgeon, actually, who's acclaimed throughout the entire country as if it wasn't a big deal.

And though David doesn't outright say it, the best that I can gather is that this is the first house that he's bought for himself, not because he wanted to start branching out and making a path for himself, but because his father didn't want to keep paying all of the bills while he sat around and twiddled his thumbs.

And that might have been a red flag to some people, but I just can't shake the fact that when he talks, it feels like the words are curling up and making a home inside of my chest; when he looks at me, I'm filled with this sense of being exactly where I'm supposed to belong. This point of no return that started almost before we officially met, a moment where we weren't able to avoid each other;where we would never be able to undo our meeting.

I do help get his system put together, pulling the wires and hooking things up; and eventually I'm not doing anything for work. I'm just sitting on his fancy leather couch, in his fancy lake side house, and we're talking.

There's something about our conversation that drives me deeper into a brewing obsession. I've been unable to not stop thinking about David these past two weeks, and now I know that I'm never going to be able to avoid it. Everywhere I go, no matter what I'm doing, it's him that will be on my mind.

And because it's him that will be on my mind, I'm almost surprised when he mentions that he needs to get going – and in the same moment, when I realize that I've just totally missed out on my next appointment.

I rush off to the front door and he follows me. Right before I turn to head for the walk, and after our unfortunate goodbyes, he snatches hold of my wrist with one hand. "Wait!"

"What's wrong?" I ask, turning to look at him. Before I can get anything else out, he's leaning forward and he's kissing me.

His hand curls around the back of my head, fingers tangling lightly in my hair, as our lips slide together. It's not chaste but it isn't deep either, something that is so terribly sensual it makes me want to just melt into a heap on the ground. I lean hard into his chest, curling one hand around his hip so I can slide it into his back pocket.

If that kiss could have lasted forever – well, it would have been the right thing. Our conversations, they were electric. But this? This combined moment of touch and interest, this shared bit of passion? It's something else entirely.

It sends sharp bolts of something intoxicating down my spine and has heat building up under my skin in these heavy sort of whorls. I want to be here forever, but we have to part ways for air eventually. My cheeks are bright red with a blush and my lips are tingling.

I ask, "what was that?"

"I just couldn't let you leave without giving you that,' says David, a smile curling over his face. "I wanted to let you know what I really thought about you." and then, "you should come back sometime, maybe without having to do the work first."

The question made my stomach flip into a knot. I lean forward again, pressing a much more chaste kiss to the corner of his mouth. "I think that I would like that."

I pull a business card out of my back pocket and a pen from my front, scribbling down my home number and handing it to him.

"Here," I say. "You should give me a call sometime."

He takes the card, smiling as his thumb swipes over the number. He tucks the slip of paper into the front pocket of his dressed down button up, and then says, "I'll do that."

And then I turn, and I head back to my car, getting in and pulling out. I have other things that I have to do, but nothing is enough to get David Holmes off of my mind.

CHAPTER TWO

Bitter Bliss
✶ ✶

Over the next three months, David and I went out on four dates. I loved him. I knew that. It spilled up inside of my chest, heat and warmth, something sicky sweet in the back of my throat. It bubbles up into being every time that we come towards each other, and then it curls out of existence when we leave. I don't like the emptiness that it leaves behind.

Even if it's only a day or two that stretches between when we see each other, it's still enough to make me feel as though my heart has been frostbitten, as though there is no return, no way back. On our first date, we get something to eat at a restaurant I would never be able to afford on my own, but he drinks so much that we have to get a taxi home. I think at first that it must have something to do with the first date jitters, or maybe just that he's got a soft spot for the sweet red wine that we had ordered to split at the table.

But on the second date, we went out to a country club. It's the middle of the day and the sun is shining. He tells me all about how nice I look, how beautiful I am – but he orders drink after drink, until I have to drive him all the way back to his pretty little house by the lake. There's no first date jitter excuse this time around and no fancy bottle of wine. There's just the two of us in a place that he knows well.

That's when I start to realize that maybe there's something wrong with David, something that should scare me off but doesn't quite make me second guess things. The connection that we share with each other is too strong and too all consuming. It sinks into my bones and my heart. It etches itself onto the insides of my ribs.

His name is a brand on my soul that will never heal over, and I'm alright with that.

But the third date comes around and our meal is interrupted by a woman with long red hair showing up. She plants a hand on the table right between our plates, her fingers covered in glittering rings. Her nails manicured in a way that must have cost two weeks of my entire paycheck to do.

When she leans forward, the front of her black dress gaps and shows off her tits. And they are some pretty nice ones, even I have to admit it.

David stares at her, his mouth slightly agape, eyes wide. He glances from the woman to me and back again, but neither of us say anything. We all just sit there in this sort of awkward, heavy silence.

And then finally the woman stands back up, and she flicks the long hair over her shoulder. She says, "you know what? I came over here and I was going to say something after I saw you. But I think that this is enough."

And then she turns and she leaves, but her point is made. I'm sitting there, and I know that the man in front of me is seeing other women. I know it the way that every woman can realize that their man is cheating on them; in the way that makes you understand that everything you're doing – everything that you've ever wanted – is just slightly outside of your reach.

"David?" I ask, turning to look at him. He's got a nervous expression on, and he's picked up his drink and taken a sip of it. I wonder if the white wine is going down easy after his other woman has come over.

And I end up just doing the same thing, picking up my drink and downing the white wine. It's cold but it burns a little bit on the way down, and it sits warmly in the pit of my stomach. I think that there's something about the whole situation that curls inside of me and makes me want to cry.

But I don't.

We just sit there and finish our date, and then we leave in silence.

It should be the end of things. That should be the moment that we're supposed to call it quits, that we're supposed to turn away from each other and just never see each other again. But instead, he calls me a week later and invites me out, and I go with him. I tell myself that it will be the last time, but I know that I'll keep coming around.

My heart aches for him.

It's not until this fourth date that I find myself being forced into a change. I'm waiting for him at Veranda Blue, a hot up and coming club that I think might be my favorite place in the world. It's bright and has my favorite music playing out of the speakers.

David is late.

I sit at the bar and sip on strawberry daiquiris, listening to the base thud its way out of the speakers. Thud. Thud. Thud.

Time passes. David isn't just late, he's stupidly late. I start trying to call him, but he doesn't answer. Not the first time, or the third time, or the seventh time.

Eventually, I stop calling and I just start drinking in full. At some point, I decide to stop waiting for him and I go home. It's three days past that before he calls me. David tries to apologize by saying that he was in a car accident on the way to Veranda Blue, and for a moment, I'm consumed with this grief that he might have gotten hurt.

But then a thought strikes me, and I say, "were you drinking first?"

Drinking first.

There's silence.

I insist, "David, were you drinking before you came out to the Veranda Blue?"

Another lapse of silence. Once it's clear that I'm not planning on saying anything, David lets out this heavy sort of sigh. "Yes."

I hang up on him. He wrecks his car a second time two months later, and it makes something inside of me feel as though a pot is about to totally spill over. The water bubbles and boils and splashes onto the ground, and I know that he has a drinking problem, and I know that he sees other women, but – there's this brewing heat in my chest.

Every time that I think about David, there's something more inside of me. There's a growing heat, a growing want, something more. A growing need. I can't understand how these emotions are mine. Up until now, I've always considered myself to be a steady sort of person, someone that can look at a situation and see how the world really looks.

But when it comes to David, I've gone blind, deaf and mute. All my reasoning becomes dull.

I go back again, and again, and again.

He often chuckles and says, "we have a unique bond. I always feel good when I'm around you."

"Then you should spend more time around me and less time around those other women," I tell him, meaning for it to be almost a joke and almost serious.

He just smiles and says, "maybe I will," but we both know that he won't. And he proves it. That no matter what sort of a bond we have with each other, he's not going to give up on the chance to be around other women, on the chance to have something with as many people as possible.

David's selfish like that. He's a collector of things, of people, pleasure and of love.

And when he collects something, he never lets it go again. So there's this darkness, but there's also a light. And it draws me in deeper and deeper, the way that it draws so many things and people to David. He has an aura like I've never seen on anyone else before. He wants something else, something deeper, darker, something that expands and twists, like a universe folding in on itself, and then out, and then in again.

I can't leave him though. I can't get away from his orbital field. There's a brightness in it, too, even with all of that darkness. The kind of thing that I never want to be without. The light that he gives off, it makes me remember what it was like to be happy. On and off, on and off, there was a light in the dark. I would call him sometimes and try to talk to him, though he never seemed to to have remorse.

Even without that, I couldn't bring myself to truly hate the man.

There's something about that makes you love him, despite his wrong doings. I could feel myself being pulled deeper into his grip and going there happily, a smile on my face.

I try to figure out what to do about things, to convince myself that forgetting about David is the best thing to do. People leave relationships all the time. And yet, it's hard to view this as a singular relationship that needs to be managed. Instead, I find myself considering it as a wide spreading moment – as something that is more akin to destiny.

And who can ignore destiny, when it is right there knocking on their doors? Who can ignore destiny when there is only one thing that could ever happen? Only one outcome that could ever be even remotely conceivable within the grand scheme of things?

This is the thought that continues to haunt me through the days, as one week bleeds into the next, as one call turns into the next. I think about how we are meant to be together, and how being apart feels like it picks a raw wound into my chest. If my heart was visible – if my emotions were physical – I can't shake the feeling that all of this distance and separation would have them bleeding.

Near the end of our first year of knowing each other, I decide to give it one more chance. I go over to his house. The door is cracked when I stop by.

I knock on it, but there's no answer. I let myself in, calling out, "David?"

I cross into the living room, looking it over and taking in the nice decor. He's rich, and it shows. There's a sound in the adjacent room. I didn't see anyone's car out front but David's, so I assume that he's alone and I head towards it. Why else would the door have been opened, anyway?

"David," I called out again, pushing the door open. His bedroom light is on. The curtains are opened too, and right there in the bed - yes he is with another woman again.

She shouts, startled, and throws herself off of him. The woman, a blonde, grabs the blankets and pulls them up over her chest. There's sweat on her skin and her eyes are wide, cheeks bright red.

"Jessica," says David, surprised. He reaches out towards me, but I take a step backwards, a steely expression settling over his face.

"You said that you would stop," I tell him, and then I turn and head for the front door. I can hear him running behind me, tripping over himself in his haste to get out of the bed and pull on a pair of boxers. His feet skid over the ground and he chases after me.

At the door, it's like a repeat of our second meeting. He grabs me by the wrist, stopping my retreat. "Just stop for a moment. I can explain."

I turn towards him, pulling my wrist away. I fold my arms over my chest, lips pursing together, and I tell him, "then explain. I'm waiting." He just stands there and stares at me, like he hadn't actually been expecting the chance to try and defend himself. Of course, he doesn't have anything to say. There's no way to defend his actions – there's no way to make it out as though he could do anything to justify this.

He contines to stare at me.

I stare at him.

And I came to a realization, too. This is it for me. The universe is telling me that David Holmes will never be mine, not fully and not in a way that counts. I turn, tears burning hot in the corners of my eyes, and I start making my way down the driveway, to my car. I can hear the woman inside shouting about calling a cab and going at him, calling him all manner of names.

I get in the car. David is still standing in the doorway, staring at me. No matter how much pain I have to endure, I know that this is going to hurt – I have to stand true to this decision. He was immature and was totally not fully awakened to this encounter but he knew it was somewhat special but not enough to change.

There is nothing that I will be able to do to wake him up before he's ready. I'm going to have to just leave here and endure the pain that it comes with me. I don't understand why the universe would do this to me, why it would make something so true and earnest and warm build up between us, and then ensure that I would never be able to access it again.

That I would always be missing something, because David is simply not capable of returning the bond between us, no matter how strong and fierce the connection is.

So I leave. I get in the car, backing up out of the driveway, and I just leave.

I don't look back.

I want to, but I know that if I look back, even in brief, even just once, I am never going to be able to leave. I need to get out of here. I need to.

So I don't look back, and David Holmes never calls me again and I never reached back out to him.

CHAPTER THREE

The Separation

✳ ✳

Over the next few years, my life changes – drastically. I moved from the city to somewhere a little bit smaller. I got a new job and I met a new man, but our relationship doesn't last for long. The connection just wasn't there. I kept telling myself that it would grow and form and come into being, but by the time I realized it was never going to happen, it was too late. We already had two kids together and a life of responsibilities.

Still, over time our marriage continued to go downhill. Soon, we're in the middle of a messy divorce – and somehow, I end up with both kids. I loved them. Harry is big into football and has dreams of going pro one day. The coach at his high school seems to think that he can actually do it, too. He believed he has a chance of making it onto some big team.

I don't know too much about football but I try to pay attention and learn for Harry's sake. His father had been the one to do it previously, always going to games and watching it with Harry on Sundays. But now that's all on me.

I can't decide if it's a good thing or a bad thing that his sister, one year older, Emily, isn't really interested in anything. She doesn't have any sports that she follows and she isn't apart of any clubs. She takes an interest in acting one day and that may change, but its the dreamer in her that reminds me of myself; thats just what teenage girls tend to do-be young and free. There's nothing happening in her life that seems to be a driving force especially after her father left the house. I know our divorce left her bitter and she grieved of her father and us not being together.

I keep thinking, today, we'll make a connection.

Today, we'll be able to find something that lets us really reach out to each other. Our eyes never meet, though, and Emily always seems to be a few steps away from me at any given point in time. She doesn't want to do any special. She was once interested in learning about sewing, cooking, or cleaning with me. In a strange way, it was a time when we talked and laughed at the most silly things. Now, her days are spent listening to music with her headphones on.

You would think that as the years pass and the seasons change, that I would move on. Not from my ex husband, Grady, but from David. But I don't. The pain and grief stay near as if my life was under a shadow that creeps in when I least expect. I could not escape and felt isolated because no one could understand. It was as if he lived inside me. Maybe it lived inside of him too, because though we never spoke anymore and so much time had passed by already, there was still this connection between us.I felt trapped because his well being and his ability to overcome his obstacles were intricately linked to my very survival. His bad day was my bad day and I hated it. I never really knew what was truly happening but I knew I had been down that road before. He would certainly not understand this and I knew the late nights he was with other woman, it pierced my very soul like a knife. The grief was excruciating as a mother grieving for her dying child. I lay aimlessly hoping the nightmare would end as my heart beat fiercely through my chest. I managed to think perhaps his joy could somehow be mine to keep sane. The days became longer but I became stronger. The grief could come at any moment while doing just regular everyday things but it was certainly beyond ordinary and could literally bring me to my knees; the pain inside was unbearable. His darkness brought weakness to my soul. I hoped in my heart he was well because that meant I would be well. It did get better over the years but it never really stopped altogether. The more I harbored hate in my heart, the worse I felt. It was the only way I survived was to believe he would be his best self. I continued to find solace in the simplest pleasures in life through art knowing that there was more beauty that surrounded me than the darkness that tried to overshadow it.

I remember the calls that came in silence, usually late at night, sometime after his office would be closed. I hear the phone ringing now and though there will be no one on the other end of the line, I haul myself over to the land line anyway, snatching it off of the cradle and tucking it against my ear. "Hello?"

There's nothing on the other end of the line, just silence and faintly, the noise of someone breathing.

"Say something this time," I say, my voice a low hiss. Emily is in her bedroom with headphones on, listening to whatever band she's obsessed with at the moment, but Harry is just in the living room, watching a football game on TV. I don't want them top know what's happening.

Not that there's much happening, really, because my demand goes unanswered.

"Say something you coward," I could all but spit into the line. "I know who you are and I know that you're calling me because – because you can't forget it either. So say something!"

But there are no words that greet me. This isn't the first time that I've lost my cool on the phone. Normally when I answer and find nothing but silence, I pause in silence too, and we will simply take pleasure in the rasping noises of our combined breaths.

But sometimes, that's not enough. My want for him is too great. My need for that brewing orbit that we had before overwhelms what we had been fighting over. I lose my temper. I've begged him to talk. I've threatened him. I've screamed, when the kids aren't home, and broken down crying, begging for him to do something.

To say something, anything, even if it was cruel, even if it was him telling me to never speak to him again. And it is always answered with nothing.

It might seems strange. I am letting this person call and say nothing, but I know that it's David. I can feel it. My heart skips a beat whenever he calls, and that same electric rush comes back, surging down my spine and into my fingertips. It feels, always, as though we might be able to come back and regain that connection with each other – but there is nothing to come about from it.

There is never anything done, because I know that – no matter how much time has passed, no matter how much our lives have differed over the years – he was not willing to change. I struggled to forgive which made the pain even worse.

He knew it was special in some strange way but he just wouldn't look at how his behavior had caused harm. I had enough and what a jerk, I thought. That's what I tell myself when I would slam the phone.

I can't go running back to him, because I know what will happen and I know that he simply will not realize his wrong in all this. That no matter what goes on between then and now, and no matter what happens in the coming days, he would never change.

David is an immovable force. He is a stone in the middle of the ocean that even the tide cannot seem to push away. A wall that withstands the test of time, something that even the worst storm in the world is unable to shake or move from it's foundation.

And if he can withstand all of that, then what hope do I have of ever making him view the world differently? Of ever making him understand that the darkness built up inside of him can be released, if only he just lets out a breath and let's me in?

The answer is this.

None.

David will never change unless he wants to. And unless the world cracks through in the middle, then he is never going to want to surrender. The darkness often

overshadows the light in him and his soul cries out.

I will always be stuck with the madness of his shadow and just the thought of this misery overtakes me.

The grief at this realization comes over me like a wave. Though my children are home, I cannot stop the tears from welling up in the corners of my eyes, burning hot. I clamp a hand over my mouth, trying to stifle my suddenly ragged breathing. There's something in the air that makes me feel almost sick.

In the living room, Harry calls out, "mom, who was it?"

"No one," I managed to get out, pleased that my voice actually sounds fairly steady.

Harry calls out, "are you going to come back in?"

I'm crying. There's no way that I can go in there right now. "I will, just let me use the bathroom real fast."

Harry mutters something under his breath but I take it as an agreement. I turn and hurry to the bathroom, closing and locking the door behind me, and trying to catch my breath. I pulled myself together for my kid and we finished watching the show, but it's not always that easy.

At times, I couldn't get out of bed, thinking, why am I feeling so sick yet I felt blissful? It's a melancholia that creeps into your veins and bones, that curls in your heart, that creeps into your stomach and your throat. I am so sad that I cannot get up and move, and yet so overjoyed at times that I can't even sleep.

There were times, I literally would be in tears on my knees from something outside of myself. It is such an all consuming thing that I decided something must be done about it.

So I visited a psychic. The woman inside has curly red hair and a pleasant smile. The moment that I sit down, she says, "oh, you have a strong connection with the other worlds, don't you?"

"I don't know." I sit down and tell her what has been going on, and she nods her head at me, as though she was fully expecting to hear exactly that.

"I can tell," says the woman, at the end of it all. "That you have an eternal bond that would never be broken and you need to embrace the process."

"You're crazy," I say.

She says, "you can think that if you would like, but the truth is this: I know who you are, in a spiritual sense. And I know that you will never be able to rest or find peace if you do not embrace this connection but it starts within you."

"And how am I supposed to do that?" I demand. "There's nothing there for us to build on. He won't change, and I can't be with him as he is."

The woman shakes her head. "I cannot answer that question for you. All I can do is tell you that there is a connection, and it cannot be broken. You will continue to be ailed in pain until you find a way to connect with the love within yourself."

"How do you know about that?" I demand, having not told her about the spells that I have on occasion.

She shakes her head, gesturing at her forehead. "The eye can see many things. And one of the things seen is how your connection is so strong that trying to break it has put you in a state of fervor and sickness. There is nothing that can be done to change that, save mending the connection itself. And if you do not want to mend it, you must resign yourself to continuing to let yourself battle the sickness." " Love is unconditional and you must find peace and harmony within your soul to overcome your fears as there is truly no separation between you and your other half." It is all an illusion, my dear."

She sounds insane. I pay and I leave abruptly but I can't stop thinking about the encounter. It haunts me, just as David has haunted me for years. It simply wasn't making sense. He was wrong and it certainly wasn't me who caused all this.

CHAPTER FOUR

Reuniting With Love
* *

Time passes and I find myself running into an old coworker, a man named Daniel Greene. He smiles at me and we quickly find ourselves in fast conversation. Somehow, we end up on the conversation about old loves – maybe because I told him that I had been divorced just a few years back.

Daniel shakes his head. "They just don't make love like they used to. Say, speaking of love and old things, have you heard about David?"

My heart skips a beat at just the mere mention of his name. "What about David? We lost touch when I moved."

"I'm not surprised," says Daniel. "He stopped talking to pretty much everyone after the diagnosis. I just thought that since you too used to be together, it might have been different with – what's that look for?"

"What diagnosis?" I ask, frowning. I brace my hands on the handle of the grocery cart, rocking forward.

Daniel seems surprised, his brows raising. He asks, "you didn't know?"

"I don't know anything about a diagnosis. Is he sick?" I'm suddenly thinking about the days that I couldn't get out of bed, wondering if maybe it had less to do with my own need for him on an emotional level and more to do with the fact that he was sick, and I had been picking up on that.

"He's been battling cancer for years," says Daniel, with a shake of his head. "They tried taking out the tumor when it first showed up, but it spread too far, too fast."

"What about chemo?" I ask. I'll be honest, I only know about cancer in a distant sense, in the way that most people know about it. That they are a far reaching thing, something that seldom shows the true reach of its cruelty and sickness.

This is proven when Daniel makes a face. "He went through a few rounds of it. Cleared things up the first time, and he was in remission for about four months. But I guess that kind of thing tends to come back. They tried it a second time, but it didn't do much of anything against it."

My stomach drops down into my feet and then deeper still. A wave of dizziness washes over me and I have to lean forward, clutching at the handle of the shopping cart in a vain attempt at keeping myself steady.

If Daniel notices the way that I look or how I'm acting, he doesn't say anything about it. Just clucks his tongue and shakes his head before saying, "We were all hopeful for a while, but things have started taking a turn for the worse here lately."

A female rounds the corner, about twenty years younger than Daniel, give or take a few. "Daddy! There you are. I was starting to wonder if you had gone outside for something."

"No, I was just catching up with an old friend of mine. Come here, Betsy, let me introduce you." He says.

Betsy comes over and I have to force myself through the interactions with her, letting her take my hand and give it a shake. My tongue feels leaden and every word that comes out is robotic and forced, stilted. I'm running through a script. The only thing that I can think about is David, and how he has been going through all of this alone.

The moment that they let me go, I rushed out to the car. I don't even bother to actually get my groceries, just leaving them sitting in the cart just inside of the store. It's a good thing that my kids don't live with me anymore, because I'm consumed with the need to not only call him but to go and see him.

All this time, David still has the same number. "Hello?"

"David," I say. "You sound…"

Awful. His voice is clearly hoarse and his throat is rough, but something about it still feels like an unending melody.

"Amazing," I finished.

There's a long pause. Disbelief heavy in his voice, David asks, "Jessica? Is that you?"

"It's me," I say. "It's me." Tears spring into my eyes. I feel like he knew that he was wrong, and that he had grieved just as much as I did. I felt it but I realized my own faults. That's why I called him originally, and that's how I know that we are meant to reconnect.

We stayed on the phone for almost an hour while I sat there in the parking lot, talking about everything but the obvious elephant in the room. Eventually, he needs to go take care of dinner and I really need to get home, because I am starting to get cramped and stiff from sitting in the car for so long.

But as soon as we get the chance, we would call each other again. He admits to being the one that had been calling before. "I just needed to hear your voice." "Those were the worst nights. When I was just so damn sick." I didn't want to say anything to you. I was worried that you would just come back because I was sick."

My breath catches. "Did you want me to come back?"

"I've missed you more than I thought it was possible to miss something," he admits.

I let out a watery laugh. Again, all I can think about is how badly I've missed him. How after all this time, he's finally here; he's finally gotten so close that I can almost touch him. And as soon as I have that thought, I realize that there's no way I could ever have anything less.

We talked for hours that night and then again, after that. I ended up packing most of my things. I retired the year before, and that gave me the chance to travel back to my hometown and see him again. David still lives in the house on the lake, the one that I had always thought was so gorgeous and pretty, so lovely to look at and soft to be in.

The house welcomes me back with the same open arms that David does. He brings me into the house and kisses me; and it's sweet and not, so passionate and heavy, it's as though we never left. We spent a lot of time talking about how things had been but also how things could have gone.

"I was immature," says David. "I didn't even realize it until after I got the cancer. I wasn't alone. I had friends but I realized that I didn't have you. And that made a difference."

"I just couldn't stay," I told him. "Not with you acting that way. With knowing that you wanted me to share you with other people. I just couldn't do it." I lean close, kissing him again. "But David, I never stopped thinking about you."

David says, "you got married."

"It didn't last," I told him. "We never should have gotten married. I thought that the relationship would grow, and that I would end up feeling for him the same way that I felt for you. But that didn't happen. And after we had kids, I realized that I wasn't ever going to feel the same way about anyone else as I felt about you."

He shakes his head, but there's a smile on his face. I think that he must have felt the same way, and that's why he never actually settled down with anyone else. After the first few days, though, we don't talk about the past, not really. We have too much else to focus on.

David doesn't have much future left. It's an unavoidable fact. But I plan on spending as much of it with him as possible.

I get to have David – to truly have him, the way I wanted but the years of pain was so immense. I kept it bottled inside for years. We shared our stories of our life and what we hoped and dreamed. I stayed for several months after moving in with him. They were the best four months of my life. We spent every day with each other, right up until he moved into the hospital. And then, into hospice. Even then, I would go and I see him every day, reading to him from our favorite books, and stroking my fingers over the back of his hand.

He never outright apologizes for sleeping with other women when we were dating, but he doesn't need to. I know that he is sorry, and that, on top of it all, this was a different time. That was a time when we were not the mature people that we are today. People evolve and learn. Perhaps, we both had to grow up and the time had not come when we could be together, even if we wanted to. And now, we were in a completely different time, where we could be together, where we could live in harmony and enjoy the world around us, to recognize the beauty of life.

Even if that world was getting smaller every day.

And when it got so small that I was the only one left, I was still there. I held his hand in those final moments, and when David took his last breath, well, it was like something inside of me broke. There was a snap, a cord that had been cut, a moment that could never be mended, brought back, or restored.

My breath shudders in my chest and comes out as a sob, and I stay there with him until David's family arrives. Then I leave, back out into the wild of the world, knowing that something has happened here today, and that it can never, ever be undone. The ties that have bound us have been cut.

So for the very last time, I say my goodbye to David, and I leave – this time knowing that he will never, ever return.

CHAPTER FIVE

The Takeaway
* *

Years passed by and with each season bringing in her beauty and splendor. One would think that grief gets easier to bear as time passes by, but the opposite is true, that you simply find ways to cope and find away to survive it, a least in this situation. I breathed deeply the fresh air knowing that it was never about me. I suffered so many years blaming others and never looking at why I needed him in the first place. The solution was within me to love and better myself. I had so many aspects of my own life that were shattered and needed mending.

I never married or ever had another love in my life. The pain gave me a better appreciation of what love truly meant. A love that surpasses understanding. We had a bond that I knew, without a doubt, will never come again. In my worst moments, I think about how lonely the world has become; how this darkness had spilled open inside of me, and left a festering wound. In those moments, it's like I've lost a limb.

There is a space in my life where something should exist, and nothing is there. A space that should continue to exist, only there is NOTHING. Perhaps, that was the place I needed to be all along. And though other men came and wanted to have a relationship with me, though I had the chance to try and find another love, there is no one in all the world that could hold up to or compare to David.

He was something special. I orbited him. He was a star that pulled me into its gravitational tug, and nothing in all of the world could have gotten me shaken free from it. Even after all of this time, that was still the truth. Do people truly vanish when they pass away, but I should know better. They don't go away completely. They leave behind a mark.

That is true even of David.

And when he vanished, when he died, it was like a black hole had opened up the source of that pull and swallowed it whole. There is nothing left there; an empty yawning crutch that seems to pierce through the void and into the harshness of the unknown. And in this emptiness, in this darkness, there swirl the memories of him.

I miss him. I will always miss him. I will never be able to forget him, or find another one to take his place. And there are times when knowing that I will have to live with that emptiness forever is almost too much, simply because it is this vast, dark expanse and the darkness can, at times, be too consuming.

But on my better days, that love is still bright, even though there is no one around to serve as a returning source. The love that I felt for David was not aimless, simply because he had passed away, and it was not gone, simply because there is no physical body to return it.

It would continue to exist, like the last ember from a fire, like proof that lightning struck a tree, like a fossil deep beneath the earth – it would continue to keep me warm, and to keep me company, because that is how deep our love for each other was. It became a connection that could leave me stricken when he was stricken, and leave me overjoyed when he was overjoyed; a connection that led me to almost insanity. A bond that you love and hate all at once.

In these moments – the light ones – just the thought of David was enough to keep me going. We would meet up with each other again, after all, and though it would not be soon it would be one day. During his absence, I merely had to make sure that I remembered the good points; the comfort of his warmth, the reality and understanding of the fact that I had him once, and that had to be enough.

I can now appreciate my purpose for living and I eventually find the ability to love again.

Though the grief remains, life goes on.

David dies, and I do not. For a while, I wished that I had gone with him. But then I am able to find the light again, and take joy in the fact that I still have Harry and Emily to bring me comfort. I still have others to love.

My children grow up. Harry does make it to the professional leagues, though only for a year before he tears his ACL tendon and has to retire, and Emily goes on to start her own business with her husband; a store that sells custom made baby furniture, like cradles, rocking chairs and little toy horses for toddlers to ride on.

Harry never marries; I think that his love must have been the game, and without it, he is just as aimless as I am – but Emily had a daughter, and then she had twins; a boy and a girl. They are lovely; the twins are only twelve and the oldest girl gets bolder and brighter every day.

Emily has me over once a week, and we sit out on the front porch in the late evening sun, having coffee and discussing the world at large. I never told them about David, but only because I was not certain if they would understand. I'm not embarrassed of him or my choice.

In the winter months, we sat at the table inside. I like that much less. The sun is always a blessing, once your joints start to ache. Today is a good day, not quite winter and not quite summer, that crux between two hot and too cold. The wind blows, and it sends the chimes hanging from the eaves of the front porch, a ringing and a rattling in my soul.

My eyes close. I think for a moment that I can make out David's laugh on the wind. Some days, it really does seem like he is right there with me; as though even in death we are bound to never fully be parted. When I open my eyes again, my oldest granddaughter is coming up the walk. At sixteen, she feels like she has the entire world sitting at the tips of her fingers, ready to be grabbed. She has a bounce in her step that isn't normally there. Her bright eyes land on me. "Grandma! I didn't realize that you had come by!"

"It's Friday," I tell her, lifting up the mug of coffee. "I always come by on Friday. Your mother had to run off though. Why don't you grab a cup of something, and have a drink with me instead?"

"Okay!" Mary Ann flounces into the house and a few minutes

later, she comes back out, a mug of hot cocoa in hand. "I don't understand why you drink that so late in the day. You're going to be up all night."

"I'm old," I tell her. "I'm up all night most of the time anyway."

She laughs and sits down on the other side of the table. Her expression is all smiles. I lean forward and I ask her, "and what has you so perked up today, hmm?"

Mary Ann thinks on it for a moment, and then she admits, "Grandma, what do you know about love?"

The question catches me off guard. I think on it for a moment, a soft smile spreading over my face. It's the sort of smile that Harry might have gotten, or even Emily, but Mary Ann is far too young to know the depths of such softness.

I tell her, "at my age, I know a thing or two about almost everything. Why?"

Mary Ann looks around. "Mom isn't home?"

"Oh, we're going to be keeping secrets now, are we?" I ask, a note of teasing in my voice.

She waves a hand. "No." The lie is obvious, but I don't press. "It's nothing bad anyway. Do I need to not tell you?"{

"No, no." I wave my hand at her. "You can tell me. I know how to keep a secret. Remember? A thing or two about just about everything. Let's hear what little love bubble you've found yourself in."

Mary Ann makes a face. "Love bubble?"

"Mary Ann," I take a long sip out of my coffee. My finger taps against the side of the mug. "I'm almost out of coffee. And do you remember what that means?"

"When you run out of coffee, you get up and leave," says Mary Ann, with this fond sort of sigh. "I know, granmom. I know." She leans forward then, and she admits, "I think that I'm in love."

"Are you now?" I smile at her, my lips peeling back to show off my teeth. "Are you truly in love?"

"I am," she says, and then Mary Ann launches into a story about how she's fallen in love with a boy on the debate team, and how she knows that it's true love.

I laughed and thought, you have no idea how deep love can go... one day you might, but this? This isn't love.

And I think, again, of David – and his laugh mixing in with the chimes of the bells.

The End

Did you like this book? Make sure to leave a review, then! It's the best way to help other authors continue their series!

AFTERWORD

Our forefathers knew that the greatest of these is love. Love is the divine energy that never diminishes but holds its flame to be our inner truth. It is who we truly are but we don't remember. The pain helps us to awaken to our true self and face our inner fears to learn life lessons. We are one in all heavenly and earthly creations.

Made in the USA
Middletown, DE
04 July 2024